YUCKING DISGUSTINGLY GROSS ICKY short STORIES

D0901646

BARF BLAST

Copyright © 2019 by Susan Berran

First published in 2015 by Big Sky Publishing Pty Ltd, New South Wales, Australia

First Racehorse for Young Readers Edition 2019

All rights reserved. No part of this book may be reproduced in any manner without the express written consent of the publisher, except in the case of brief excerpts in critical reviews or articles. All inquiries should be addressed to Racehorse for Young Readers, 307 West 36th Street, 11th Floor, New York, NY 10018.

Racehorse for Young Readers books may be purchased in bulk at special discounts for sales promotion, corporate gifts, fund-raising, or educational purposes. Special editions can also be created to specifications. For details, contact the Special Sales Department, Racehorse for Young Readers, 307 West 36th Street, 11th Floor, New York, NY 10018 or info@skyhorsepublishing.com.

Racehorse for Young Readers ™ is a pending trademark of Skyhorse Publishing, Inc.®, a Delaware corporation.

Visit our website at www.skyhorsepublishing.com.

10 9 8 7 6 5 4 3 2 1

Library of Congress Cataloging-in-Publication Data is available on file.

Cover design and typesetting by Think Productions
Cover and interior illustrations by Pat Kan

Print ISBN: 978-1-63158-335-3
Ebook ISBN: 978-1-63158-338-4

Printed in Canada

Yucky, Disgustingly Gross, Icky short Stories 2

BARF BLAST

SUSAN BERRAN

FOR YOUNG READERS

<u>WARNING</u>

Ok, so hopefully you're ready for some more yucky, disgusting, gut-wrenching stories, but this is the last time I'm going to warn you— it gets reeeally, *reeeally* gross in there. So if you have a weak stomach, close the book, put your hands over your eyes, and run away screaming now . . .

If you are brave enough to read on, you might want to grab a bucket just in case!

Mel . . . always xx

Contents

YOU CAN CHUCK "UP"

BUT CAN YOU CHUCK "DOWN"?

I want you to think about this for a second
... Where were you the last time that you
barfed, chucked, chundered, spewed, threw-
up, up-chucked, puked, vomited, or just plain
old got really, ***really*** sick? Were you sitting
on the toilet after eating a bunch of totally
gross, grey, snot-like oysters, or on a boat
swaying up and down, up and down, up and
down, ***uuup*** and ***dow—bluuurrrrrr!***

What did it look like? Was it full of chunky
chewed-up veggies and stringy meaty bits?
Or was it smooth and soupy and runny?
Or maybe it was a little bit of everything all
mixed in together?

How did it smell? Like last night's curry
made with extra spice? This morning's eggs
and bacon? Or an awesome fragrant mixture

4

of all the meals you ate over the last three days, all mushed together to create an unbelievably gross stench that knocks you out colder than a charging rhinoceros?

Worst of all, how did it taste as it sped from your stomach, raced up your throat, shot past your cheeks, and flowed across your tongue like oatmeal before landing on the carpet—as every one of the 10,000 teeny, tiny taste buds that cover your tongue's surface were coated with the disgusting mixture, before it finally exploded like a massive cannon blast from your mouth? Thank goodness your taste buds get replaced every two weeks!

And finally, where did it land? Did it slam into the tiny bucket that your mom gave you—you know, the one so small that

5

the spew shoots up the sides and right back at you. Or did it splash onto the floor like a massive tidal wave at the beach?

Or maybe your vomit was like the "sprinkler," exploding in every direction as you twist and turn trying to figure out which way to run. You know when you thrust your hands across your mouth, desperately trying to hold it in, until a huge pressure forces it between your fingers, propelling it across the room, over the furniture, up the walls, and onto the ceiling, where you'll still be finding dried, yellowy spots of vomit for weeks.

Maybe you made one final, desperate bid to stop the disaster by pressing your hand even harder across your mouth, sending the

final flow spraying from your nostrils like a fireman's hose.

But for most people, throwing up is very simple and quick—go to the toilet, kneel, hug the bowl, chuck-up, flush, rinse out your mouth, and you're done. But hang on, did they chuck-up or did they just chuck-**DOWN?**

Why is it that every time someone talks about vomiting they say you threw up or chucked-**UP?** It's really weird. I just don't get it!

Why? Because you definitely chucked-**IN!** In the toilet, in the bucket, in the kitchen sink.

Or you chucked-**OVER!** Over the walls, over the room, over anybody standing within three feet of you.

7

Or you chucked-**ON!** On the floor, on the furniture, on yourself!

Eewwww!

Of course, if you did the "sprinkler" and your spew hit the ceiling, well then *tah dahhh,* congratulations, you hit the jackpot and you most definitely chucked-**UP!**

So you see, we can chuck all over the place, not just **UP**.

Now I have an idea. After you've finished reading this book, I want you to bug your parents with this annoying little question: If you can chuck-**UP**, can you chuck-**DOWN?** Let's see how smart they are.

And by the way, the last time *you* chucked . . . did you **chuck-*up*** or did you **chuck-down?**

• • •

The last time I barfed all over the place like a supersonic tidal-wave was after I'd eaten some weird sort of food at a creepy little restaurant.

The whole family had decided to go out for Mom's "special" birthday dinner. Every single one of my aunties, uncles, and cousins came along for the "big event."

We were supposed to be eating at a fancy-shmancy restaurant that my Uncle Roy said was, *"Owned and operated by a young, fun, couple who create incredibly delicious international food. The restaurant is situated in the heart of a lovely family area, at the end of a quaint street with a wonderful children's play area inside . . . blah, blah, blah."*

Well that's what he droned on about for at least half an hour. (We found out afterwards that Uncle Roy had last visited the restaurant something like seventy years ago!)

After Mom spent three hours trying on dresses, shoes, jewelery, *and* changing her hairstyle a dozen times, she was finally ready to leave. So I zipped to my room, chucked on some jeans and a top while Mom was in the bathroom, and off we went.

By the time we finally arrived at the restaurant, the rest of the family were waiting impatiently by their cars. The street was barely lit as most of the street lights were smashed and hanging loosely by a wire, banging around in the breeze.

10

As we stepped from the car to greet everyone, we noticed that this "lovely family area" looked more like the "land of graffiti" and was surrounded by half-demolished buildings. It also smelled as if the entire city had its sewage being pumped directly into the street.

Allowing Uncle Roy to take the lead, we all quietly followed along down a narrow, dark little alleyway crowded with overflowing garbage bins. We had to step around the piles of crap lying outside the front entrance of every doorway we passed. Scrawny, cross-eyed cats that looked like they'd stuck their tongue in an electric power socket, and their tail in a blender, were scratching amongst the rubbish. Lots of *very* **large**, grey rats darted from bin to bin.

We finally arrived at the very end of the alleyway; a dull "open" sign above the ancient wooden doorway flickered every time a bug exploded in the electric death-trap "bug-zapper" hanging right beside it. Everyone was shooting weird looks back and forth to each other and then across to Uncle Roy, as if to say, *"Are you sure we're in the right place? Is this really the 'amazing' restaurant we'd been promised?"* But the glasses he was wearing were either totally covered with dirt, or he was looking through a time machine, as he was all smiles and pretty excited—almost skipping along in anticipation, as the rest of us became more and more worried about what might be lurking behind the restaurant door.

As we nervously entered the "restaurant," a small, rusty bell scraped across the top of the door, and made a sound like a key being scratched down the side of a car, to announce our arrival.

We stood inside the entrance, quickly scanning the room.

"Wow, that's a nice big aquarium with lots of *fi*. . . ." Aunty June trailed off as she realized the fish had a life vest of mold covering their **upside-down, bobbing bodies.**

"Look at the wonderful artwork covering the far wall," Aunty Denise said.

"Nope, that's cobwebs," Uncle Leon remarked casually.

"I love the mood lighting," she cooed.

"Dirty lights," Uncle Leon shot back.

"The plants look nice and healthy."

"Plastic!"

"Nice soft carpet."

"Mold growing on the tiles!"

Aunty Denise gave up looking for things to like, but Uncle Roy was still smiling like he'd just won the lottery. "It hasn't changed a bit," he announced loudly and proudly.

What!? Was he blind? We made a tight little family huddle, as if to keep us safe, when suddenly, without warning, stepping out from the shadows, our waitress emerged.

She looked like some sort of *veeeery* wrinkly **Oompah Loompah!**—a little old lady who must have been at least a hundred years old, hunched over and twisted like some sort of human pretzel.

Although her eyes were barely open, she seemed to be staring at the bunch of plastic plants in the corner behind us. "This way," she mumbled. I thought to myself, if someone sneezes, she's going to blow away. But she continued shuffling along, moaning and groaning with every step, as she hobbled towards our table.

It took an hour to get from the front door to our seats—well fifteen minutes at least, but it sure felt like an hour! We took a step . . . and waited. Another step . . . and waited. Another step . . . and waited. Another step . . . and waited. Another step . . . and wait . . . **OMG** *move!!!*

There were only four other tables in the place and the only other customers were a young couple sitting in the far corner. It was pretty obvious our table was the one set for twelve people, so why couldn't she just point to it!?

By the time we finally got to sit down, I was totally starving! I'd even skipped lunch just so I could pig-out on dinner. But while the others were looking at the menu, I was

looking through the open door that led to the kitchen. It looked like our waitress's husband was the chef and he looked *twice as old as her!* I could see his very long, grey, wiry nostril hairs glinting under the light, fluttering around his nose with every breath.

He was sitting on a small, wooden stool in front of the stove with one bare foot resting up on a box in front of him. He didn't seem to notice us sitting in the restaurant as he continued intently reaching forward and clipping his cracked, yellow toenails. I could hear tiny dings and splashes every time a toenail flicked up, shot off the range-hood and landed in a cooking pot on the stovetop.

Eeeeewww!

The old man finally, slowly, pulled a fluffy sock over his foot, thrusting two toes straight through the holes in the material. He started to shuffle about the kitchen while poking and prodding his long, bony fingers into his ears, wiggling them about and—*thoop*—pulling out big globs of **yellowy, green ear-wax.** He wiped the wax across the front of his apron, which was already covered with what looked like a lifetime of earwax, and started poking those *same* fingers into every single pot and pan on the stove. He then shoved them back in his mouth, creating a bridge of mouth slime stretching from his finger back to his mouth and back into the pot. ***Nooooo!***

"Ah, Mom," I tried to get Mom's attention—but of course she was way too busy talking to everyone to listen to me.

I continued to watch as the chef started preparing the meals for the young couple. He tossed a slab of meat onto the bench and started searching about the drawers for utensils. His nose was running like a tap. Every now and then he lifted his apron up to his face, blew his nose, and swiped his arm across the top of his mouth to wipe the extra snot away with his bare, hairy arm.

"Umm, Mom," I tried again, but still no response.

Now the old guy was slapping the meat with his bare hands because he obviously couldn't find the cooking utensils and was scratching his head in between slaps. He was scratching so hard and fast I thought his hair was going to suddenly burst into flames. I could actually see the hair and dandruff raining down onto to the steaks like his own special selection of secret herbs and spices. Maybe I should tell Uncle Roy exactly what was in some of those "amazing flavors" he raved about!

"Hey Mom, you might want to see—"

"Don't interrupt!" Mom shot back, now starting to look annoyed with me.

Meanwhile, the little old Oompah Loompah waitress had finally shuffled over to deliver our drinks on a tray. But she'd taken so long, and was shaking so much, that the glasses were already half empty, the bubbles gone, and the tray was a swimming pool by the time she reached us. She then spilled ***the other*** half when she lifted the glasses off the tray and placed them down in front of us.

20

As she slowly began to shuffle away again everyone was yakking and laughing so loudly that they didn't notice there was now only about three mouthfuls left of their drink. Now, Uncle Roy was calling out for another round of drinks! ***Really!?***

I was still anxiously watching the chef, who was now getting ready to chop up the vegetables. He'd lined up a bunch of carrots, corn, and some other weird green veggies . . . although I wasn't sure if they were actually green or were just moldy. He took out his top false teeth, placed them on top of the vegetables, held them there with one hand and started whacking down on top of them with the other—*wham wham wham wham wham!* It was as if he was using a stapler to put a heap of paperwork together. There were veggie chunks flying in every direction—bouncing off the walls, dropping from the ceiling, and rebounding all over the kitchen!

"Hey Mom, I *reeeally* think you'll want to see—"

"I've told you, I'm talking!" Mom spat back at me.

The old man finished "chopping" the veggies, which were now mostly all over the filthy floor, and popped his teeth back into his mouth. He slowly bent down and used a dustpan and brush to pick up the chunks of food from the floor before tossing them into the cooking pot.

"Mom! I *reeeeeeeeally* think you need to see—"

22

"If you interrupt me one more time!" she screeched. "Why don't you go and play in the children's corner?"

Ummm, because I'm not four! And I was pretty sure the "children's corner" was actually the toilet cleaner's corner because it was three square feet with a tiny seat, a mop, and bucket ... *Hey, so that's where the cooking utensils were—in the mop bucket!*

Ok, fine, Mom, I tried! So while everyone else decided what they were going to eat, I sat back and continued to watch the chef as he scratched his head, picked his ears, scratched his butt, picked his nose, scratched his armpits, picked his fingernails, and did heaps of other gross, disgusting stuff. There was no way, no way on Earth, that I was going to eat **anything** that he'd made or touched!

Just then the little old lady came shuffling back with her pen and paper, ready to take everyone's order. As she wrote the orders down, I quickly took another look at the menu. I was looking for something, anything, that was out of a packet and could be shoved in the microwave so that I knew the old guy wouldn't be touching it. But of course there was nothing. It was all totally weird, icky, strange sounding food that I'd never heard of before.

"Try the oysters in snail sauce," Mom said.

"Or the snails in oyster sauce?" the old waitress suggested, as I sat cringing lower and lower in my seat.

This was a nightmare. I was totally starving, but every time I looked across to the kitchen, the chef was picking something new on his body and scratching another bit with his other hand. I was *sooo* going to spew . . .

"I'm not hungry," I lied. I kind of figured that my stomach could wait a little while longer because I knew there was birthday cake after dinner. I was sure the cake would come from a cake shop so I would just pig out on that!

I watched as everyone chowed down on their gross earwax covered steaks, false teeth mashed veggies, and food spiced with dandruff. Uncle Roy seemed to purposely

25

wait until he had a mouthful of food before starting each conversation and was spitting tiny chunks of food and phlegm across the table. I sat there quietly trying not barf.

The dinner seemed to take forever and my stomach was rumbling louder than a volcano about to erupt by the time everyone had finished their meals.

A few minutes later, the little old woman appeared at the kitchen door, holding Mom's birthday cake. Finally! With the candles flickering in the dull light it looked incredible. It was huge. I couldn't wait!

Everyone sang "Happy Birthday" as the waitress hobbled towards the table with the cake. She was *sooo* **slow!** We sang "Happy Birthday" again as she kept shuffling and the

candles continued to burn. We sang it two more times, and then everyone gave up and went back to talking for what seemed like five minutes.

By the time the waitress finally made it to our table the candles were puddles of wax on top of the cake and there were only two tiny flames barely flickering for Mom to blow out. But I didn't care. I was starving! And the best part was that everyone else was totally stuffed full of their disgusting dinner so I was the *only one* who wanted cake. Awesome!

I ate a huge piece, then a second even bigger piece . . . and a third . . . and a small fourth piece just to finish off. I must have eaten at least three quarters of the cake all by myself! I eventually sat back in my seat, content and completely full. I was barely able to stand when it was finally time to head home.

And as we left the restaurant, Mom and the others thanked the little old lady and her husband for such a wonderful and memorable evening, and especially for *making* the birthday cake **themselves! *Nooooo!!***

So it didn't really surprise me when I started to feel a bit weird and queasy on the drive home. Where we lived was roughly a thirty minute drive out into the countryside. We drove over heaps of hills that twisted, turned, and wound up and down, over, under, around and around—all the way home. The further we went, the worse I felt.

"Mooom, I feel sick," I whined.

"Look out the windows," Mom replied, as

she usually did when I felt carsick. Yeah, like looking out the windows is somehow going to magically stop my guts from exploding. My gut doesn't have eyes, Mom! And anyway, it was totally dark. What was I supposed to look at!?

"Mooom, it's getting worse."

"We're nearly home," she gave me a desperate glance. I knew she was fibbing.

We continued to wind through the hills, going around one way, back the other way, and around another way, and back the other way, and *blllu* . . . around and around *blllllu* . . . and around and around and around and . . . "Mooom I'm gonna . . ."

"Just a bit further! We just hit the edge of town."

"I don't think I can hold . . . *blllllu* . . ."

29

"Hang on! We're in our street!"

"I'm not gonna ... *bllllu* ..."

"Hang on! There's our house!"

"I'm gonna ... *bllllu* ..."

"Hold on! We're in the driveway!"

Bluuurrrrrrrrrrrr!

What is it with parents?! We try to warn them. We try to do the right thing. We tell them a hundred times on the trip that we need to pee or puke. "How bad?" they ask. "Really bad," we reply. Then we have to go all the way up to ***really reeeally reeeally bad!*** But still they ask, "Can you hold it?" "No!" we yell.

And then when your bladder or guts bursts all over the place they get all like "Why didn't you tell me it was that bad?" ***Arghhh!***

What is it that they don't understand about "I *reeeally* need to go **NOW!**"? And they reckon *we* don't listen!

Bluuurrrrrrr!!

The car screeched to a halt in our driveway. I had my hands tightly pressed against my mouth, trying to hold back any more vomit from escaping. But it was useless. Chunks of yesterday's dinner, including carrots, peas, and corn forced their way through the gaps betwcen my fingers.

Bluuurrrrrrr!!

Yellow, slimy liquid instantly sprayed smack into the back of Mom's head, parting her hair before flowing down her neck and squishing between her back and the seat.

Bluuurrrrrrr!!

31

Another load slammed into the back of her seat right in front of me, before bouncing straight back to splash all over me as well.

"Couldn't you hold on for just a few more seconds until we were out of the car!?" Mom whined.

If I wasn't so busy barfing like a massive human volcano, I would have said something like . . . "Yes Mom, yes. I *could* have held it in a bit longer. But I thought it'd be way more fun to chuck-up all over myself, the car, and you because I love the smell and feel of warm vomit running down my face *so* much." Geez, as if! (Although seeing Mom's face in the mirror as the back of her head was smothered in vomit *was* pretty cool.)

32

Mom finally yanked on the handbrake, flung open her door, took off to the side of the house, grabbed the hose, turned it on, ran back down, opened my door, wrenched me out and began spraying water all over the car seats to wash the chuck off of them so they wouldn't stain. The water sent bits of corn, carrot, and other food chunks shooting straight back at us like little veggie bullets, belting into us at warp speed—man, they hurt too.

Then Mom started to hose herself off! Hello? Kid being sick here! What about me?! So I'm left standing there covered head to toe with slimy, disgusting puke and after what seemed like forever, Mom turns to me and says, "So are you starting to feel any better?"

33

Hmmm, how can I respond to that without getting in trouble for really bad swearing? I say nothing and hold my chuck-covered hands out assuming Mom would finally start hosing *me* off. But instead, she hands me the hose and heads straight for the house saying, "I feel so gross. I'm going in for a shower. And you need to hurry up as well, it's past your bedtime!"

Great, thanks Mom!

To make matters even worse—if that was at all possible—after I quickly soak myself and begin to follow Mom into the house, she turns around and tells me that I have to totally strip off before I can even think about coming back into the house because I'm dripping

spew. Aha, so she didn't want me dripping puke and water through the house but it was fine for me to die of pneumonia.

At least it was totally dark so the neighbors wouldn't see me. I quickly started to strip off near the front door ready to do the quick nudey dash through the house to the bathroom. Suddenly, I heard Mom call from inside, "Oh sorry it's dark. I'll turn on the floodlights for you."

Woop woop woop woop woop woop

"Oops, sorry, that's the alarm. This one's the light switch."

Noooooo!

Great. I reckon within a split second every house in the street had someone peering through their window to see why our alarm was screeching—just as a gigantic floodlight lit up my backside like a full moon as I desperately stumbled into the house.

Shivering uncontrollably and covered in goose bumps the size of eggs, I raced straight to the shower.

I was amazed at how many chunks of food and puke were hiding on me. Bits of food kept dropping off me as I washed, so I had to squash them down the drain hole with my toes. By the time I finished my shower I was still feeling crappy, so I headed straight to bed. But Mom was certain that I just needed to eat something before I went to sleep to help me feel better again.

I crawled into bed, curled up, and felt like I was ready to die. Ten minutes later, Mom came strolling into my bedroom with a few slabs of toast smothered in butter saying, "A piece of toast will make you feel heaps better."

37

"But I *don't* want anything to eat," I moaned.

"Trust me, toast is the best thing for you."

"But, I don't feel good."

"Just one piece of toast," Mom persisted.

"I don't want anything."

"Just try to eat it. You'll feel better."

"I feel sick again."

"Because you haven't eaten your toast!"

"I don't want any toast."

"Eat it."

"I don't want—"

"Eat it!"

"I feel—"

"Eat it!!"

What was wrong with her!? Mom just wouldn't let up.

"I'm going to be—"

38

Bluurrrrrr

"Quick, get to the toilet!" Mom yelled.

I dove out of bed.

Bluurrrrrr

My chuck splattered across the bedroom wall beside me as I stood up.

"Run!" Mom screamed in my ear.

I staggered towards the doorway—*Bluurrrrrr*—spraying the door with vomit as I went through.

"Don't stop," Mom bellowed from behind me. *Bluurrrrrr*. I staggered through the living room. *Bluurrrrrr*. Spewing across the TV. *Bluurrrrrr*. Throwing up along the couch. *Bluurrrrrr*. And the coffee table. *Bluurrrrrr*. Up the steps. *Bluurrrrrr*. I stumbled along the hallway. ***Bluurrrrr***. Trying to step over the vomit I was chucking-up in front of my own feet. ***Bluurrrrrr.***

"Put your hands over your mouth!" Mom yelled desperately.

Bluurrrrrr. It forced its way between my fingers. So now instead of one huge dump in front of each step, it was spraying all over the place like a powerful sprinkler! ***Bluurrrrrr.*** Up the hallway walls—both sides! The ceiling, the floor, the lights, the pictures hanging on the walls—nothing was safe!

"OMG! Hold your mouth closed tighter," Mom screamed in horror. I quickly forced both hands as tightly as I possibly could over my mouth. I knew the toilet was

40

just ahead. With the door closed, I now had both hands busy trying to hold spew in. *Bluurrrrrr.*

Ewwwwwww.

Nothing came out of my mouth that time . . . it all came out through my nose!

If you've ever had vomit come out of your nose, or "nose barfed," you'll know what I mean. It burns! And it's even worse when the veggie chunks burst out of your nostrils like machine gun fire!

I nose-barfed all over the toilet door, but it bounced straight back towards my face. I ducked. Mom didn't. She caught the whole lot. *Splash.* Right in her wide open mouth.

"In the toilet! In the toilet!" Mom was screaming in total meltdown as she continued spitting out my veggie chunks.

With one hand still tightly covering my mouth, I reached out and tried to turn the toilet door handle. But with slimy spew now coating the doorknob and my hands, it just kept slipping. Suddenly, Mom's arm shot through from behind me to open the door.

She shoved the door back so hard that the door handle on the other side smashed, embedding straight into the wall, making a nice neat hole through the plaster. I dove forward, lifted the toilet lid, took my other hand away from my mouth, and . . .

Hey, whadya know, I was empty. Not one more drop came out, and I felt pretty good

too. Of course I told mom that I still felt sick and *reeeally* weak so that I could have another shower and go straight back to bed— after all, there was no way I wanted to clean *that* mess up.

For the next three hours, I could hear Mom washing walls and lights and pictures and ceiling and cupboards and carpet and doors and everything else. She washed my bedroom, the living room, the stairs, the hallway . . . and every now and then I heard Mom go ***Bluurrrr*** into a bucket that she was dragging along with her.

Yep, there's nothing else in the world worse than cleaning up spew—especially someone else's. Maybe she should have a piece of toast. :)

So you see, I chucked-up, I chucked sideways, I chucked over, I chucked under . . . and I definitely **chucked-DOWN**.

WHEN YOUR NOSE "RUNS"... WHERE DOES IT GO?

PART ONE

Ok, so here's an interesting little story from a few years ago when I was just a little guy at day care. There I was just sitting around in the sandpit. I was hanging out, minding my own business, making the world's coolest and most awesome sandcastle, with these excellent flags

48

made out of leaves, wicked seashell windows, and tiny little acorn horses that I'd made to go with the King's popsicle stick guards.

Next thing I knew, this solid, dorky looking kid with long, black, curly hair, and who was missing most of his "baby" teeth, comes waddling over to me. As his shadow fell across my castle, I looked up, squinting towards the sun and said "Hi" but he just stood there in his bright orange, baggy pants and Spongebob Squarepants t-shirt, staring at me with a strange look on his plump, freckled face.

I wasn't sure if he'd heard me or not, so I said "Hi" again.

"Urgh," he grunted, barely moving a muscle. That's when I noticed the line of dribble slowly sneaking from the corner of

his mouth and sliding down toward his chin. I kept working on my totally fantasmagorical sandcastle, but from the corner of my eye I was still studying the string of drool ever so slowly sliding, stretching, and winding its way down his chin until . . . *sssslurp* . . .in the blink of an eye he sucked the slobber back up into his mouth and it was gone.

"Do you wanna play?" I asked.

"Urgh," he shrugged. Then another long string of dribble started slowly stretching down from the corner of his mouth, across his chin, and winding through his minefield of freckles. This guy was acting weird!

But then I had an idea. I figured that if I could get him to play with me, then I could use his string of drool to make an awesome

50

moat around my castle and a flowing river through the little town I was making.

But he still refused to play. He just stood there staring and grunting and sucking his dribble back up through his teeth when it reached the tip of his chin.

I was just about to give up asking him to play, but then I was blinded for a second as the sun bounced off something else on his face. It was so big and bright. Why hadn't I seen it before? Obviously I'd been so busy focusing on all of the dribble action that I hadn't noticed the massively giant "thing" on his forehead. It was humongous! Was he growing a second nose on his face? Or had I just discovered a brand new planet in our solar system, attached to his head?

As I continued to stare, I realized it was the world's biggest, fattest, slimiest pimple! It was the size of a pancake stack, shoved smack-bang in the middle of his greasy forehead. It was the Tyrannosaurus Rex of pimples!

I was wondering if it would suddenly open up and swallow his head whole. I was completely hypnotized by the throbbing mountain of pus in front of me and it seemed to be growing larger every minute. Hey, if that thing erupted, there'd be thick, yellow pus raining down over the entire sandpit, the daycare, or even the town!

"So do you wanna play?" I asked one final time, trying to ignore the disgusting sore on his head.

I decided to try and appeal to a boy's

mutual dislike of girls. "I only like playing with boys. Girls are gross!" *Hey, I was only three and three quarters!*

The strange kid sucked in the latest line of dribble hanging from the corner of his mouth and began to lower his thick, bushy eyebrows that were weirdly joined in the middle and ran from one side of his head to the other, and glared at me.

"It'd be cool having another boy around to play with." I tried again.

He stepped towards me but now his eyes had narrowed even more, squinting as his eyebrow shaped into a sharp arrow pointing straight down the middle of his face. He made another loud grunting noise.

I realized he actually looked really peeved

off with me for some reason. He was just
about to say something to me when one of
the carers called out "Samantha."

Wait, isn't that a girl's name? Oops!
Hmmm, now I knew why she was grunting
at me as if she was about to smoosh me
into the ground like a snail being sat on by
an overweight elephant . . . because she **was**
about to smoosh me into the ground like a
snail being sat on by an overweight elephant.

He . . . I mean *she* turned and started
heading off towards the other girls. But when
she saw the carer turn around and begin to
wander away, *Samantha* suddenly turned
back and began to run . . . straight towards
me! ***Arghhh!*** She was going to kill me for
calling her a boy.

She was going to slap me about with her dribble and snap my head off with her bare hands! I was doomed. She was coming right at me like some sort of super-charged tank! She was about to rip right through me like a charging rhinoceros when suddenly she stopped.

She stopped dead in front of my face, with only my award-winning castle standing between us. I could feel her warm, smelly breath and hear the gurgling of drool washing about inside her mouth. I could also see the whitehead on top of her monstrous pimple throbbing angrily, ready to blow.

Samantha then kicked the crap out of my awesome sandcastle! *WHYyyy!* Sand smacked into my face and was flying through the air in every direction, including into my eyes and up my nose. Seashells shot into my mouth, plugged my nostrils, blocked my ears, and stung my eyes! She stomped my poor little acorn horses into the ground, shredded the guards, and sent them splintering in all directions.

Then Samantha leaned forward and stuck her creepy, oily face only a centimeter away from mine—*pewww*—her breath was worse than the backside of a dead skunk that had exploded when it was run over by a steam roller!

But then, just as I thought she was about to open her mouth, shove me in, and swallow me whole, she blurted out, *"Eeewwwww! Your nose ran!"* before turning and running away to play with the other girls.

"What? **Arggghhhhh!"** I screamed at the top of my lungs before leaping from the sandpit!

"My nose ran?! Where did it run to?!" I threw both hands up to my head, covering the middle of my face so that no one else would see the gaping hole. Beneath my clasped hands I could feel a hard lump where my nose used to be . . . bone?!! It had to be my nose bone protruding from my skull! I could also feel a thick, cold liquid slowly rolling down across my face. Blood?

"**Arggghhhhh!!**" I took off, racing around the grounds like a cheetah with its butt on fire.

All the kids were staring at me as I bawled my eyes out, blubbering at the top of my lungs. Why had my nose run away? Maybe it had entered a nose race? Yeah, maybe it was running with heaps of other noses in a face-parts marathon to prepare for the Olympics or something.

I was really worried my face was now going to have this massive gaping hole right in the middle of it until my nose decided to come back home! And what if my eyes dropped down and rolled out of the hole in the front of my face? Or my brain slipped out and got jammed halfway? And what really scared me

was that if my brain dropped onto the floor, I had no idea how to *wash it*.

Great! I'd be like the backside of a mole rat ... really ugly, no brains, and lost in the **dark!** And it was all Sucky Samantha's fault! Obviously, when she leaned in really close to my face, her super bad breath and greasy face scared my nose and made it leap off and run away! And it was now *running* around, somewhere, all on its own, and I had no idea where to even start looking for it! I had to find my nose fast, because I could feel myself getting more and more confused by the minute as my brain slowly slopped about!

I ran around the playground, kicking about toys, drinks, and anything else in my path. Through the sandbox, using my feet and elbows to shove things about, searching every nook and cranny, while at the same time screaming and trying to hold back tears. "Nose. Stop running. **Come back!!**" I yelled at the top of my voice. I was totally freaking out! I had to find my nose.

One of the carers finally came over to find out what was going on. I cried while still clasping my hands across my face. "My nose ran away and now my face is leaking and my brain is dropping out!" I screamed at her through the flood of tears.

(Hey! I was still only three and three quarters!)

The carer tried to convince me that my nose hadn't "run away" just "ran." Of course, I didn't believe her ... until she took me

60

inside and put me in front of the mirror to prove to me that I didn't have a great big massive hole in the middle of my face. As I slowly brought my hands down from my face, **thick yellowy-green boogers** overflowed from my cupped hands and escaped between my fingers like long green yoyos. Thin long strands stretched all the way from my face to my hands like gooey spider webs. There was so much snot that some had started to go crusty, gluing my hands together.

Geez, I was going to get that Sucky Samantha!

Over the next couple of days, I watched Samantha like a hawk. I saw her massive gigantasaurus sore in the middle of her forehead grow bigger and redder. By the end of the week it was the size of a small planet and pulsing bright red with its humongous, creamy whitehead ready to erupt. It seemed to be taking on a life all of its own too. I could swear it was breathing . . . and watching me. I could see the zit pushing upward, as if the thick whitehead was trying to burst through. It was payback time!

I waited till nap time when all the kids were fast asleep. Once the carers thought we were all sleeping soundly, they quietly tiptoed out of the room and off to the staff room to drink coffee, munch chocolates, and watch TV. That's when I went to work. I threw back my "blankie" and shoved "Floppy," my stuffed cat, under my arm. I quietly slid down the zipper on Floppy's belly that usually

stored my pajamas and took out the thick, red marker that I'd hidden in there and snuck over to Samantha and **_veeery_** carefully drew a **great big butt** around her pimple!

When Samantha finally woke up she had this huge, bright red "butt" and massive whitehead right smack in the middle of her forehead, leaking, festering, slimy, and very smelly pus from her pus-butt mountain. Payback was awesome!

And the best part was that butt-mountain stayed on her forehead for nearly two whole weeks.

Hey, I was three and three quarters, how was I supposed to know the marker was permanent . . . I couldn't read!

PART TWO

65

So anyway, when your nose does "run," I don't know where it goes, do you? I definitely think there should be some sort of "nose race," or world record for the biggest bucket of snot. Actually, I do know the guy that holds the world record for "longest unbroken booger." He's in the "Extra Ginormous Book of Incredibly Awesome and Unbelievable World Records."

But I also don't get why your nose "runs" instead of "walks." Nobody says, "Hey get a tissue, your nose is 'walking'." Did someone just decide that snot runs because it likes to exercise and stay fit? Or maybe it runs to escape? Yeah, that's probably it. Your boogers are trying to escape before they get eaten!

We've got this kid at school, Toffee Thomas.
He's totally stuck up and thinks he's *sooo* cool
but he's actually repulsive.

If there was a world record for fastest "nose
picker," Toffee would win easily. I reckon he's

got a snot factory instead of brains. He must have. No one can have that much snot just in their nostrils. Unless their nostrils are the size of buckets! Toffee's always got his fingers zipping in and out of each nostril like ferrets whizzing in and out of their burrows.

There was this one time when one of the other kids, Abbey, went to borrow Toffee's eraser, which was sitting on his desk. She walked up behind him so she didn't see him happily picking away. She reached across his shoulder to pick up the eraser when *sploosh* Toffee raised his snot-loaded finger towards his mouth but slammed it into Abbey's arm instead. I thought he was going to bite off a chunk of her arm. Wow, did she scream. She spent the rest of the day scrubbing her arm clean.

Toffee just sits in class with his elbows leaning on the desk so that he can continue his picking and eating non-stop for hours. Once he gets going there's no stopping him. It's just a blur. A crazy ballet of fingers dipping in the nose sauce at supersonic speed. Each finger goes up and in, and before it even gets to his mouth, another finger from the other hand is already on the way into the other nostril.

One time he was going in and out so fast that when the teacher said to take notes, he grabbed his pen and accidentally shoved it right up into his nostril—*wham*—*"Arghhh."* Geez, that would've hurt! He jammed it in so hard that it must have embedded in his brain! They had to get the school nurse to yank it out with pliers! It was hilarious.

It can be very hypnotic once you start watching him for a while. Kind of like watching one of those zombie horror movies, when the zombies start chewing on someone. It's so disgusting and gross that you desperately want to turn away, but you can't. Hey, here's a thought—zombies are the foulest creatures to ever walk the Earth: the living-dead, the disemboweled deceased, the decomposing departed, the walkers, the rotting corpses with maggots chomping on their flesh—but, have you ever seen a zombie sticking one of his loose flesh fingers up his nose, wiggling it about, and then yanking it out to eat his boogers? **Noooo!**

Because picking your nose is even way too gross for zombies. What does that tell you Toffee?!

So every single class, Toffee is tugging at his nostril taffy. And it's fun to watch, because at least twice a day he falls asleep, jamming his fingers right up into his nose and straight into his brain. And the moment he does it, everyone knows because the second his fingers block his nostrils—*shnort!*

But when we have gym, that's when everything gets really gross—and it's definitely no longer funny! If we're playing tennis, it's fine until it's Toffee's turn to serve. He chucks the ball up into the air with his snot-covered hand and *smashes it* right at me! I hit the ball and *sploosh* the ball sticks to my racquet like a velcro glove! At the same time, slithers of snot come splashing through the racket and splatter me in the face—the ball just sort of hangs there like a slimey yoyo on my racket until *I* have to grab the snot covered thing and pull it off! What's fair about that? It's not my snot!

I love playing soccer—until Toffee, who is our goalie, stops the ball, picks it up in his snot covered hands, and kicks it to me. ***Boof.*** My boot is engulfed in a flood of snot as I try kicking it, but it instantly returns, tethered to my boot by strands of his snot until I sit down and yank it off. ***Eeewww!*** Surely that's worth a red card?

And then there's basketball. Well, I'm sure by now you get the picture. Me attached to the ball, hanging from the basketball ring, surrounded by Toffee's snot. Toffee and any sport equals disaster of unhygienic proportions.

72

So basically no matter what sport we play, there I am, soaked in snot, and no one else seems to notice or even care! Not the teachers or the other kids. No one!

Toffee is addicted to snot. He just sits around all day, twirling the slimy, stretchy snot around his fingers like cotton candy on a stick and then into his mouth it goes. Other times stretching and twanging it as if it's some sort of musical instrument that he continues playing until it snaps.

So, why does your nose "run"? To get away from people like Toffee Thomas of course!

THE STREAKER

75

PART ONE

Beep beep beep **beep beep** *beep*

The alarm clock screamed at me with its deafeningly high pitch that makes me want to rip my ears off my head and stuff them into a blender—I really hate that thing! One of these days I'm going to shove a massive firecracker in its battery compartment! Then blow the thing into a gazillion and one pieces, feed it to the dog, burn the dog's poop, and rocket it to the center of the sun. Yep, that ought to do it.

Then I smelled it. The disgusting stench and the putrid odor of morning breath. It was kind of like sticking your nose into a laundry basket full of dirty underwear and socks. What a way to wake up. But then I remembered, today was the day! *"Extra Ginormous Book of*

Incredibly Awesome and Unbelievable World Records," here I come.

I'd been dreaming of this day for ages. From the first moment I'd come up with my awesome idea, I'd been patiently waiting for my opportunity. Trying to imagine what it would be like to have hundreds of thousands of people—well at least a few thousand . . . maybe a few hundred . . . actually probably more like a hundred—with their mouths hanging open, staring wide-eyed in total gob-smacking amazement at me, glued to my every move. They would be blinding me with lights as their cameras honed in to capture history in the making. I couldn't wait to take in the cheering, the applause, and no doubt, the looks of sheer amazement.

Today was going to be the most incredibly awesome, fantastically amazing day of my entire life. And, just like the humongous pus-filled zit pulsating away on the end of my nose, I was ready to explode forth and fulfill my destiny! Nothing was going to stop me. Fame and fortune awaited and I was going to make sure that no one would forget this day, ***ever!***

I realized early on that I needed to be super fast, agile, and very, *very,* **very** flexible. Like every other great athlete, I had dedicated myself to the task with lots of preparation and training, spending day after day, week after week, stretching and running as much as possible . . . totally naked of course, just to make sure everyone was paying attention,

as I prepared for the biggest event of my life. I reflected on my rigorous preparation.

I had wanted to make absolutely certain that I was at the peak of physical fitness. So I ran and ran and ran. Only a little at first. Short quick dashes outside when no one was around to watch. The last thing I wanted was to have a heap of people making weird faces, staring, laughing, and pointing at me. I'd been spotted before running around with nothing on and people treated me like some hideously gross monster. Parents would turn away, quietly telling their children not to stare.

Some days were harder than others as I tried to keep up with my grueling schedule. But I soon found that I was beginning to actually enjoy the training sessions. I began to increase my speed and distance, always trying to maintain complete secrecy so that no one would try to stop me. The main reason I didn't want anyone to see me out training was if someone guessed what I was up to, they'd probably try to beat me to the record! Or worse still, turn me in. I wasn't going to let that happen. This was *my* chance at a new World Record!

Of course it would have been way easier if I had asked for a bit of help, but I couldn't risk it—what if my "helper" turned traitor and tried to wipe me out!? Yes, I knew I had to do

this on my own and I'd only get one shot at it. Just one chance because . . . well let's just say, I don't think anyone is going to let me hang around with nothing on long enough to take another shot at it.

But as go-day drew near, I began to grow suspicious that **someone** knew what I was up to and had told on me. I could tell that people were trying to stop me from training. If I even looked like running outside, someone would suddenly point at me, sneering, laughing, or making cruel, weird, twisted faces, and nasty comments. It was even worse at school. I could feel the burning gazes of the teachers and kids staring at me. They were ready to snap like the worn-out elastic in Grandma's undies if I even looked like I was going to run. It totally sucked!

But it was really Kevin, my number one evil archenemy, who I needed to hide from. He's a bully, and for as long as I can remember he's always picked at me. Whenever he thinks no one is watching, he starts poking and pushing me. It really hurts too! Sometimes if a teacher catches him he'll get in trouble. We've even been to the Principal's office, but that just ends up in a bit of a lecture for him to leave me alone. Kevin always sucks up and says "Sorry, I won't do it again" and that's it! Of course, the minute we get out the door Kevin starts having a go at me all over again!

Yep, Kevin was the one person that I really worried might find out and wreck everything

for me. If he knew what I was planning, there was no way that he'd let me go for the record.

Like the other day; there I was right in the middle of training, finishing one of the longest runs I'd had in ages, when suddenly there he was. He made sure no one was about, and then started poking me with his long bony fingers and taking huge digs at me. Where were all the teachers when I needed them?

Then things started to get *really* bad. Mom and Dad spotted me running. They didn't say anything to me directly, but that night I overheard them talking.

"We have to put a stop to it! And he has to wear something warm when he goes outside!" Mom said all in a fluster. "We need to get

this out of his head! If he keeps running like this we may as well take him to hospital right **now!"**

I knew I was constantly being watched, but I wasn't giving up. After getting caught by Mom and Dad, I did all of my naked training under the cover of darkness; stretching inside where no one could see me before sneaking out into the freezing night air. I'd take one quick peak around to make sure the coast was clear before zipping out and taking off like a rabbit with its fluffy little tail on fire. The colder it was, the faster *I* was.

After a couple of weeks my "Incredibly Awesome and Unbelievable World Record" was looking better and better. I just had to stick to the plan and run as if I had a banana

taped to my butt and there was a starving gorilla on roller blades chasing me.

Part Two

Finally, my big day had arrived!

The annual school play was the perfect setting for my record-breaking attempt. I was going to break the record right there on stage, in front of as many people as possible. I wanted an audience *full* of witnesses with cameras so that there was absolutely no way anyone could question the result. It was perfect!

You see, every year our crappy little school does some totally lame, boring little play like . . . "Eat Your Vegetables Or You'll Die," "Cross The Road at The Crossing or You'll Get Smooshed And **Die!**," or "Be Nice to Everyone or **You'll Die!**"

Yep, totally lame!!

And this year there was a new one, "Never

Ride a Crocodile or **You'll Die!**" Wow, worst play **ever!** But I didn't care. There would be heaps of people to tell the incredible story of my unbelievable record for generations to come. Children would sit at the smelly feet of their great-grandfathers, glued to every word pouring from their cracked, yellowing lips. And for all those unfortunate people who didn't attend the play tonight, they would forever regret not being in the audience to witness the historic event.

The play wasn't due to start for a while, but already school kids were gathering in the dusty old town hall. Behind the heavy, red curtain they formed a tight little huddle as the principal, Miss Nada, began to give us her long, boring speech about "Giving it your best shot!" and "There's no 'I' in 'team'." Well *derrrr!* Wow, it's two minutes till show-time and we're having a spelling lesson?

But if she didn't hurry up with her speech, there could be a few dead actors, or people vomiting from standing next to the thick, furry armpits of "BO" Brett. Yep, anywhere near BO for more than about five seconds was a disgustingly gross and deadly place to be. He smells so bad that the poor kids that sit next to him in class are always pretending to have a cold just so they've got an excuse to stuff great wads of tissues up their nostrils. And everyone answers the teacher's questions the second they are asked so he doesn't shoot his arm up in the air and release his deadly toxic stench into the classroom.

I pitied the people in the front three rows of the audience because BO was the "Band Conductor" and he was going be raising his arms and waving them around all night long! *Eeeww!*

Miss Nada continued to prattle on and on. "Every student is just as important as the next one. Even getting my coffee and broccoli sandwich at lunch time is just as important as playing the lead role."

Yeah right . . . *not!*

Everyone knows that Zombie Marty got stuck with the "coffee making" job because he's totally useless at anything else. We call him "Zombie" because he wanders around with this blank look on his face. Kinda like he's wandering about searching for a brain.

He has this little trail of dribble from the corner of his mouth rolling down his chin and his face is almost completely covered in these festering, red, scabby sores. His sister, Feral Cheryl, got the job of sandwich collector because she acts about as bright as a dead glowworm dipped in black paint, sealed in a black box in a cave at the bottom of the ocean. I overheard the teachers talking and saying that Zombie and Feral might have picked up their behavior from their dad. On the school camping trip last year they'd seen Zombie and Feral's dad stick his hand into the fire to "see if it was warm enough."

Yep! The jobs they'd been given were important alright—important to make sure they were kept as far away from everyone else as possible! And as for me? I was in the lead, naturally. And now I was about to become famous! My record would go down as one of the greatest moments in our town's history! In fact, it might actually be one of the greatest moments in our state's history . . . or even our *country*. Fame was near.

PART THREE
FINALE:

High above the stage hung a very ordinary looking clock. Its simple, round face was worn and faded from the many decades that had passed. As the thin, aging silver hands struck seven, the large, wooden auditorium doors squealed open like a violin being played by a goat, before slamming back against the outer crumbling brick walls.

The hall began to fill with parents, teachers, friends, relatives, and other invited guests. They were all shuffling along like a herd of confused sheep, wandering down the aisles, treading on toes, nudging and squeezing past each other with a fake "sorry" while they looked for their correct row. It was fun to watch people scooching along over strangers' laps to search for their allocated seat, all the

while talking loudly on their cell phone so everyone could see how important and cool they were.

Other people were talking even louder to friends who were standing all the way across the other side of the hall. I don't know why they didn't just wait until after the show to yak to each other about all the boring stuff they were doing!

Chairs were being scraped and screeched along the hundred-year-old, wooden floorboards like fingernails drawn down a dusty chalkboard with the evil, ear-piercing sound echoing throughout the auditorium. There were the people elbowing the person beside them "accidentally" as they stood by their seat and shuffled about trying to remove their

oversized jackets and put down their hand-bags filled with junk.

Finally, the last people to enter the hall, the town mayor and his wife, were escorted to their VIP seats at the very center of the front row.

Gradually the lights faded away, blanketing the room in complete darkness and this was quickly followed by the loud *"shushing"* from people all over the hall. Suddenly, a bright white spotlight split the darkness in two like a bolt of lightning and directed everyone's attention to center stage. The last scattered coughs and throat clearing from around the audience spat out as phones clicked off and finally everyone fell silent.

Behind the red, faded stage curtain students were sweating like pigs slowly roasting on a

spit. BO Brett stood below the stage at the very front of the audience and immediately raised his arms high above his head to prepare the band for the opening piece. The entire front three rows instantly went puke-green and a heap of them started making puffy, throw-up cheeks.

But then, just as we were about to step out onto the stage, there was Kevin and he started poking me—again. I knew he wouldn't be able to leave me alone! Miss Nada screeched out "Kevin!" in a high-pitched whisper and gave him the evil eye. Every kid on the stage spun around and looked straight at him. He was *SO* embarrassed. Excellent!

The curtain began to open. The flowing red curtain parted up the center and swept across the stage. The music began and BO Brett waved his arms about, swishing them back and forth across the air, sending the stench of a thousand sweaty camel butts wafting through the auditorium. And as the lame play unfolded there were the usual **burps**, **farts**, coughing, and crying babies in the audience.

You could almost hear everyone yawning with boredom and elbowing each other to try and stay awake. The boredom was occasionally broken by the sound of heavy footsteps clumsily racing along the dark aisles, towards the main entrance, as people couldn't hold their stomach contents down any longer and needed to vomit because of BO's stench.

I'm pretty sure they puked all over the front doorstep before tiptoeing slowly back to their seat with a handkerchief mooshed over their face to try and keep out BO's deadly odor.

By the time the curtain was raised for the second act, most of the band was ready to dash for the door and puke, so the teacher taped BO's arms down by his sides. He had to conduct the rest of the play holding the baton between his teeth.

The play was a total **dork-fest!** But there I was right in front of everyone, in the lead!

Forty minutes later, the spotlight finally softened, fading away for the last time. The curtain closed, signaling the end of the show, and was followed by an eerie silence. I think most people were either asleep or passed out! But after the awkward silence, suddenly the audience woke up and erupted with enormous applause like a herd of stampeding, tap-dancing elephants. Mothers were weeping

with pride at seeing their kids prancing around. Dads whistled loudly to *pretend* they liked it as well, but really they were just celebrating that it was over so they could finally go **home!**

Behind the curtain everyone quickly took up positions, ready to step forward, take a bow, and receive the air kisses from the parents. In the darkness, I sneakily began to do a few stretches. The lights came back on and once again the curtain swung open. The students all joined hands to form a long line and stepped out to take their final bow. Naturally, because I was in the lead, I was right at the very front, center stage, beside Miss Nada. Everything was going according to plan.

As the applause died down, Miss Nada took the microphone and began to thank everyone for coming, **blah blah blah**. And of course she thanked the teachers for all the stuff that no one really cares about, *rant rant rant,* and praised the performers, particularly Kevin in the lead role because he was ***sooo*** sick with the flu . . .

Hey, I was in the lead! This was it! Show time! Lights were on, cameras were rolling, and every pair of eyes in the hall was staring in my direction. As I summoned up every tiny bit of strength I had, everything seemed to fall into slow motion. It was now or never! *Extra Ginormous Book of Incredibly Awesome Unbelievable World Records,* I was on my way!

104

I squiggled about, wriggling, twisting, squiggling, then suddenly . . .

aahhh . . . aahhh . . . aahhh . . . aahhh . . . chooooo

"Bungeeeeeee!"

I flew out of Kevin's nostril totally naked! Racing like a slimy, green booger-bullet with a rocket up its butt. The second the cold air hit me, I ran even faster!

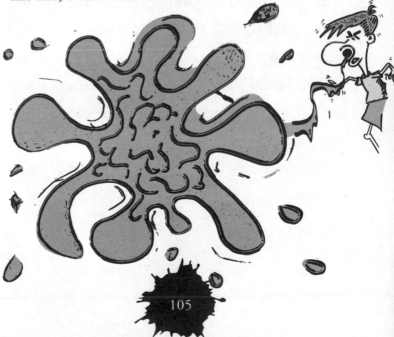

I flew off the stage, over the band, and straight towards the front row of the audience like a gross, green javelin. I kept stretching further and further. I was straining with everything that I possibly could to run as far as possible *without* breaking away from my hairy, dark nostril home.

Within seconds I was only centimeters from splatting right between the mayor's eyes. His eyes bulged like ping-pong balls and went cross-eyed staring at me as I came closer and closer. I was barely millimeters away from his thick, bushy monobrow when, *Twang!* I was sent flying backwards like a slime covered yo-yo. Back towards home, back to where I'd come from, back towards Kevin's wide open nostril.

Yessssss!

I was sure I had gone way further than any other booger had ever gone before me!

I could feel Kevin's face burning red with embarrassment as gravity took over. I fell downwards, bouncing about uncontrollably before being left to hang only millimeters from the filthy stage floor, dangling from the nostril that I'd been living in all my life.

As Kevin's face tightened in shame, the pressure inside his head came close to a massive brain explosion, I could feel the pressure of the pus building up inside the humongous zit at the end of my nose home. It was going to blow!

Suddenly *ppthttt ppthttt ppthtt.* **Ppthttt ppthttt pthttt.**

Minuscule droplets of thick, yellow pus burst into the air from the huge festering volcano. The pimple erupted, spewing its contents across the stage and all over Miss Nada and the audience. Wow, pus fireworks for my achievement!

Everyone in the front row turned an even weirder shade of green as the droplets of pus fell from the air like some sort of yellowy-green shower. **Woo *hooo!*** Eyes were popping, jaws were dropping, and girls were throwing up—actually pretty much everyone was throwing up. It was **awesome!**

The new *"Incredibly Awesome and Unbelievable World Record"* for *"**LONGEST SINGLE STRAND OF** Booger**—NOSTRIL STILL ATTACHED"*** was all mine!

And somehow I knew that it was going to be a **very, very** long time before another booger could beat that!

Incredibly AWeSOMe and 'UNbeLievAbLe WorLd Record'

LONGEST SINGLE STRAND OF BOOGER... NOSTRIL STILL ATTACHED

THE TINSY-WINSY, ITTY-BITTY STORY OF

SIR REGINALD BERNARD

PUSBUCKET XVIII

. . . THE ZIT!

110

Part One

This is the tinsy-winsy, itty-bitty story of the average-sized Sir Reginald Bernard Pusbucket XVIII. Wait, hang-on, it's actually the **average-sized** story of the tinsy-winsy, itty-bitty Sir Reginald Bernard Pusbucket XVIII—aka the zit!

Once upon a time, not very long ago, there lived a family of tinsy-winsy, itty-bitty, pus-filled zits living deep under the dark, damp, hairy forest of Left Armpit, on the sacred land of The Great Ranga. The Great Ranga was the name for one extremely obese, hairy, super old and exceedingly large, but very happy, orange Orangutan who inhabited the city zoo.

Living in the city zoo was absolute luxury for The Great Ranga. It meant that at least six times a day, three hundred and sixty-five days of the year, he was fed a very large wheelbarrow full of all his favorite foods.

And because he didn't need to run away from predators, climb trees to forage for food, wander through the forest searching for shelter, or basically do any sort of strenuous

activity at all, he just lazed about day after day, week after week, month after month, and year after year, getting **bigger** and **bigger** and **bigger!**

It wasn't long before The Great Ranga's hairy skin was so loose and so flabby that every fold of skin sat on top of another fold of skin that had yet another fold of hairy skin beneath it. These layers of skin made it look as if he was wearing a bright orange fur coat about twenty-four sizes too big for him.

The Great Ranga's huge bulbous face seemed completely squashed between his ballooning cheeks that were held up by five double chins sitting on top of his gigantic belly. His arms and legs hung off him like fishing poles; looking as if they were twice as long as they were supposed to be. When he lifted his arms the skin unfurled and flew out like the massive sail of a yacht being released into the wind. But there was absolutely no chance of him blowing away—not with that gigantic butt acting as an anchor.

Poor old Ranga looked like a giant, hairy, orange potato the size of a double-decker bus created by some crazy scientist. With his bright orange, long, wiry hair carpeting his body he looked like a *very* deranged monkey.

His rolls of fat made him the perfect hotel for thousands of families of sweat-loving, pus-filled zits. His left armpit was the Buckingham Palace of The Great Ranga's body.

Sir Reginald Bernard Pusbucket XVIII was taller and thinner than his brothers

115

and sisters. He was also the eldest and yellowest in his family. He had thirty-nine brothers and nineteen sisters to annoy him. The Pusbucket family had been born and raised under Left Armpit for more than one thousand, nine hundred, and thirty-six generations of zits . . . which is about thirty-five Orangutan years.

Sir Reginald had always known that being the eldest son meant that someday he'd have first pick of where to live and raise his own family. He could see why his great great great great great great great great great great great grandparents had chosen to live under Left Armpit—it was heaven. For twenty-four hours a day the whole of Left Armpit was blanketed in complete darkness—blacker

than the ear of an elephant stuck in a box, in a cave, five miles underground. And the smell was awesome—a wonderfully toxic, putrid smell that got grosser every second due to the total lack of air. It smelled like a putrid mix of moldy cheese, sardines, and rotten meat wrapped up in sweaty socks.

Oh, and the food under Left Armpit was absolutely out of this world! The whole Pusbucket family loved soaking in the moist, warm, salty sweat of The Great Ranga—sucking up the delicious, liquid body fat. It was the perfect place to put on weight and grow pus. Yep, life didn't get any better than this for a **zit!**

Although . . . there was one small, teeny, tiny downside. Every now and again The

117

Great Ranga would stretch his arm up. It was only for a minute or two, but it was just enough to let in a slither of sunshine. These moments were dreaded. They never knew how long the sun would be heating them up, drying them out, and giving them fresh air . . . *eeeeeewwww!* But it was a small price to pay for such a luxurious home.

Yep, life was good. But with another seven brothers and sisters expected to pop-up any day now, Reginald Bernard Pusbucket XVIII was ready to move to his own little patch of paradise and start raising little Pusbuckets of his own. It was getting pretty crowded in Left Armpit so he considered moving away from the rest of his family; maybe even as far away as Inside Right Elbow.

To get there, it was a few days travel around Back of Neck and down the treacherous steep descent of Right Bicep mountain but it was still largely unpopulated—although there was was much more of a chance of sunshine there and nobody wanted that!

Of course, there were other far more dangerous areas of The Great Ranga, like Butt Basement. It was a great place to visit for a holiday with a wonderful stench from the massive butt-gas explosions and the best place for food and luxury resorts. But living in Butt Basement was risky. It was constantly being scratched and picked by The Great Ranga—and others. He was always digging those monstrous sausage fingers with razor sharp nails on and around his butt, and if

one of those fingernails came anywhere near you, **_sploosh_**, the zit's head would be ripped clean off in one swipe.

You see monkeys are all totally and utterly disgusting! If you sit back and watch them they all sit around in pairs, on the ground, in the trees, or anywhere else they want to, and spend hour after hour picking each other's fleas and scratching their own butts! Two minutes later, you see them picking their nose _and_ scratching their butt! What's even worse is that they use the same fingers and whatever is on the end of those fingers goes straight into their mouth.

So it can get very dangerous for a zit living in Butt Basement. When the shadow of a finger falls across Ranga's butt, a siren

sounds and the zits only have a few seconds to get below. If they aren't able to suck down under the skin they're in deep trouble. Entire families have been wiped out. The attack can last a few seconds or a number of long, painful hours as he scrapes those fingernails across his tough, leathery butt skin, along the deep dark Crack Canyon and across Buttock Cheeks. Like a destructive tornado, The Great Ranga's razor-sharp fingernails catch and rip heads off, exploding brains high into the air. What a horrible way to go!

For some time, Sir Reginald had been dating a zit on Left Buttock Cheek in Butt Basement, named Daisy May Posterior. Every chance he got, Sir Reginald would slither off beneath The Great Ranga's skin, over and under fat-fold after fat-fold, under his blubbery belly, around his bulging waist, down and around to Left Buttock Cheek and his girlfriend, Daisy May.

Now, Daisy had fifty-two brothers and forty-nine sisters, making a lot of Posteriors. Luckily, The Great Ranga's butt cheeks were so wide that there was still plenty of room for more Posteriors down there.

But unlike the Pusbuckets of Left Armpit, the Posteriors hadn't lived in their home very long—only a few hundred generations. Their family had originally come from under Right Armpit and were one of only a few families that had escaped the "Great Infection Injection."

All zits have heard the terrifying tale of the disaster that claimed so many families. The

story has been passed down from generation to generation in the hope that it will never happen again. But even more chilling was the legend of "The Golden Tunnel." The strange story that told the tale of some zits that had escaped the Great Infection Injection of 1939 and found the long lost "cave of eternal fat." But they were never heard of or seen again.

The legend goes that somewhere, far, far away on The Great Ranga's body, there's some humongous crater that leads into a deep, dark cave. The myth goes on to say that the cave is so deep that it goes all the way to the center of The Great Ranga and although no zit has ever proved it, it's said that the tunnel actually goes all the way through and out to the other side to another almost identical cave and crater. But best of all, these caves are meant to be absolutely, totally overflowing with **pure gold**! Pure, oily fat gold. It's believed that by sucking up the waxy gold, a zit can live **forever!**

But Sir Reginald didn't see how there could be any place on The Great Ranga better than Left Armpit and Daisy May agreed. She couldn't wait to leave Left Buttock Cheek! Sure, she loved sucking up the massive gas leaks and butt eruptions, but she'd felt those massive sharp nails scrape right by her so many times, and lost a lot of friends and family as they were scraped and squeezed beneath The Great Ranga's fingernails—then watched in horror as they were sucked out of there. Gone in one slurp.

But Daisy's parents didn't want to have their whole family slither back up to live under Right Armpit again. At least not for a few more hundred generations anyway. You see, living under Right Armpit was once *the* place to live. A thriving, sweat-filled, stench-ridden, wonderfully hairy place. Zits had lived under Right Armpit since just after the birth of The Great Ranga. It was pretty much the birthplace of all our forefathers. Generation after generation lived and thrived in the sweetest, sweatiest place, free from sunlight. It was the place that famous zits like Captain Pimpernel, Joan of Acne, Leonardo Da-Zitzi, and Christopher Colonpus ventured out from to find new sweaty, smelly lands to raise future zit generations.

These explorers returned having founded incredible places like the Grand Canyon (which later changed its name to Crack Canyon), Nostril Hollows, Belly Button Burrow, Waist-Band Bend, The Great Spinal Highway, and the eight Toe-jam Valleys of Left and Right Foot.

But as well as these successful explorers, there were also many brave zits that went in search of new sweaty swamps and hairy forests that just completely disappeared and were never seen or heard from ever again.

It was on one of Christopher Colonpus' expeditions around Neck Fat that he found the diary of Captain Pimpernel beside a single, thin, dried-out, yellow chip of pus. The faded, tattered diary spoke of some wonderful paradise he'd named The Golden Tunnel.

It told of a massive crater that wound its way down to a cave which then led to a long winding tunnel. Apparently, it became narrower the deeper they went, eventually leading to the center of The Great Ranga. The diary told of the tunnel being lined with thick, goopy gold that would keep a zit's pus **yellow**, **slimy,** and **young!**

The diary said that Captain Pimpernel had wanted to return and lead others to The Golden Tunnel but his team had refused to go. Now with Captain Pimpernel gone, and the pages too faded for any further detail, or any sort of map, The Golden Tunnel faded into history forever.

Of course, the legend grew with each generation. Some zits thought that the diary held the ramblings of a drying out, shrivelling zit half out of his mind and the team had just slowly dried up and withered away. While others believed that the party may still be there, alive and well.

Many others have tried to find the mysterious cave leading to The Golden Tunnel

over the generations and, sadly, many haven't come back. Those that do make it back home again are usually crazy and almost completely dried-up from trying to cross Cheek Plains and Gut Desert.

Everyone knows that it's crazy to even try slithering under The Great Ranga's cheek. It's bathed in sunlight all day, everyday and even at night it's still dry and pretty clean. And even if you're lucky enough to come across a drop or two of sweat, there's no way that there's enough to make it all the way across! But every now and again you still hear of some twit zit that has to be saved because they've gone and tried to be a hero, exploring and searching for The Golden Tunnel. **Seriously!**

129

Anyway, so Right Armpit *had* been the perfect place to live and where almost every zit is believed to have originated from. But none of that mattered when The Great Ranga's massive infection hit. It was barely noticed at first. A little bit of extra saltiness in his body fat, a tiny bit more fungus around each hair follicle, and just a little smellier than usual—*yummy.*

The zits that lived there just thought that The Great Ranga was happy, and that life under Right Armpit was just getting better and better with every generation. But they were wrong. During the Great Infection Injection, zit after zit and family after family of zits began to gradually turn green.

Zits were slowly losing their firm, red shape. Many zits began putting on massive

amounts of weight and spreading out widely at their base. Every day they were seeing a progressive change that they couldn't seem to stop or even slow down.

The Great Ranga's hair under Right Armpit became an overgrown, thick forest. But then the final stage of the infection hit. Suddenly the zits' lovely, shiny, solid "whiteheads" began to gooify, turning a deep grey with fuzzy, green fungus tufts of mold growing on top. By the time the zits realized what was happening, the fast-spreading epidemic had taken over and it was too late.

The few families that had listened to their gut instinct and sucked down and slithered away at the first sign of fungus were lucky. Unfortunately though, only a few had evacuated.

131

The vast majority had stayed and didn't have the strength to do anything but wait for the inevitable end.

And as the infection got worse, the zits' pulsating whiteheads soon became bulging, creamy, grey-colored bowling balls getting bigger and bigger, their pus getting greener and greener. Within mere days of being infected with the mysterious disease, they'd become so ill that panic started to spread across the land. They had no idea how or where the sickness had come from, but worst of all, there seemed to be no cure.

The only thing they did know for sure was that the fast-growing fungus was rapidly smothering each and every one of them. No more zits came to the land, and none left.

Meanwhile, the zits that had evacuated and resettled on The Great Ranga, eagerly awaited any news of their loved ones

It's said that just before the end of the infection, zits were up to *sixteen* times their usual size and as green as The Great Ranga's boogers. Their bulging, grey whiteheads were like massive beach balls, enormous and throbbing like a ticking time-bomb about to explode. Stretching to the absolute limit so that their skin could hold their pus in. Stretching, throbbing, s t r e t c h i n g, throbbing, s t r e t c h i n g when suddenly, ***thoop!*** zits began to **explode!**

It was a disaster of epic proportions, it was horrible. Zits were erupting all across Right Armpit. Their gooey, creamy, thick pus was

133

spurting out all over the place like alien volcanoes. Splattering as each explosion set off the next one like a domino effect. One after another whole families of zits were wiped out, splattered in every direction. A fine sprinkle of rain gently wafted along through the air, as whatever was left of the zit families floated away.

Thoop Thoop Spttt **"Arrgghh!!"** *Spttt Spttt Thoop!* **"Arrgghh!!"** *Thoop* **"Arrgghh!!"** **Spttt!** *Thoop Spttt Thoop* **Spttt!** *Spttt!*

Almost every single zit that stayed behind on Right Armpit at the time of the Great Infection Injection exploded into pusy green oblivion, leaving nothing behind but tiny tufts of their final fungus. There were only two zits that survived to tell the tale of what really happened.

134

Close to total exhaustion, they told of how The Great Ranga's arm had slowly lifted. Massive folds of skin fell downward like a bed-sheet hanging in the sunlight. The sun's warm rays poured down onto those still fighting but barely alive. Then an enormous sharp, shiny tube appeared from above and began speeding straight down towards them.

It was jabbed right into the center of Right Armpit and a flood of strange, clear liquid was plunged into The Great Ranga's body. The Great Ranga had been injected with something!

Within days, Right Armpit began clearing up. The fungus forest began to thin and the smell and sweat returned back to their usual level—still gross but not quite so bad.

And although still weak, the pus of these two survivors slowly began to regain its golden color.

Although many generations have passed, many were still worried about the injection infection, and there were only a few zits prepared to head back to Right Armpit. And who could blame them?

Luckily for Sir Reginald, Daisy May's parents had decided to move their whole family from under Right Armpit only a few hundred generations before the infection. If they'd waited just a few more days then they'd probably have been done for as well and the two would have never met.

Part Two

137

Sir Reginald Bernard Pusbucket XVIII and Daisy May Posterior were married and began their new life together under Left Armpit. They joined their names together to start their new family . . . the **Pus-butts.**

But as time passed—about thirty minutes— Daisy May found it harder and harder to be so far away from the rest of her family. So together, Reginald and Daisy decided to leave Left Armpit and make a fresh start in a new place closer to her family.

The following day, Sir Reginald and Daisy May Pus-butt slipped away and found a nice place just around the corner from Right Buttock Cheek on a pleasant little sweaty patch in Crotch.

Two days later, Reginald and Daisy May were the proud parents of eighteen healthy growing zits. By the end of the week they were grandparents to just over three hundred and twenty more and a month later they were the proud great great great grandparents of over five thousand, eight hundred, and seventy-nine teeny-tiny developing pimples.

They lived happily in Crotch, enjoying an area that was sweatier than the butt of a sloth, stank like the rear-end of a warthog sitting in sewage, and was darker than a bat living in an elephant's trunk.

Yep, it was absolutely perfect!

139

The Author

Yep, it was gross, disgusting, and just plain icky ... but ya can't say I didn't warn ya. Hope you liked it.

See you soon in ... ***"Yucky, Disgustingly Gross, Icky Short Stories—Butt Blast"*** Happy reading.

Seeya

S.B
Susan
www.susanberran.com

OTHER BOOKS BY SUSAN BERRAN

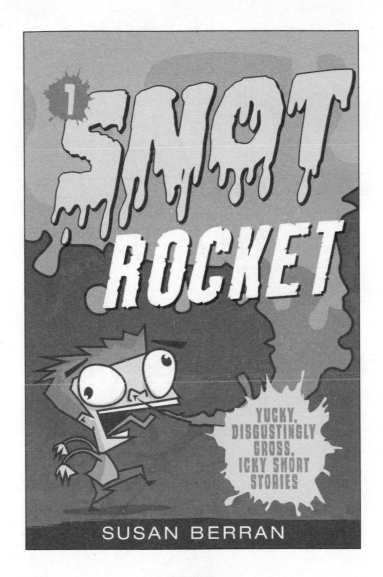

SNOT ROCKET

YUCKY,
DISGUSTINGLY
GROSS,
ICKY SHORT
STORIES

SUSAN BERRAN

YUCKY, DISGUSTINGLY GROSS, ICKY SHORT STORIES

SUSAN BERRAN